A Dog Named Rush Limbaugh
(Welcome To Life 101)

"So clear I remember these words when first we met.
So great I feel their meaning."

A Dog Named Rush Limbaugh

Welcome To Life 101

A MAL-C Book

This
book is
dedicated
to the
life
force
of the
universe.

A Dog Named Rush Limbaugh

Author's Note:

This book's inspiration is due, in part, to M.A. Laser's profound and thought provoking illustrative interpretation of Aubrey Beardsley's "John" taken from his illustrations for Oscar Wilde's story of "Salome", 1907 edition.

CONTENTS

A Dog Named
Rush Limbaugh

– 1 –

"HTAED!* HTAED! ARE YOU THERE?"

(*Htaed is pronounced 'tade')

So clear I remember these words when first we met.
So great I feel their meaning. Though
I will admit, at this time that I was quite
startled and afraid, when first I heard this voice.
I had never dreamed that such a creature existed ... and
therefore, had never expected to see one such as this
— especially in the dead of night.
I can remember that I was fast asleep …
dreaming the kind of dreams that I used to
dream, but what the dreams were about
— I forget.

_____

(You must keep in mind that this happened a
long, long time ago. And knowing that I do
pride myself on my memory ...
I do hope that you will forgive me
for not remembering.)
It was a night when everyone was asleep.
It was a quiet night.
The wind was blowing gently and
the air was sweet,
fresh and balmy. It was a good night to sleep.
Some nights are so hot that all one does is
toss and turn. And some nights are so cold that
they turn one's feet into icicles ...

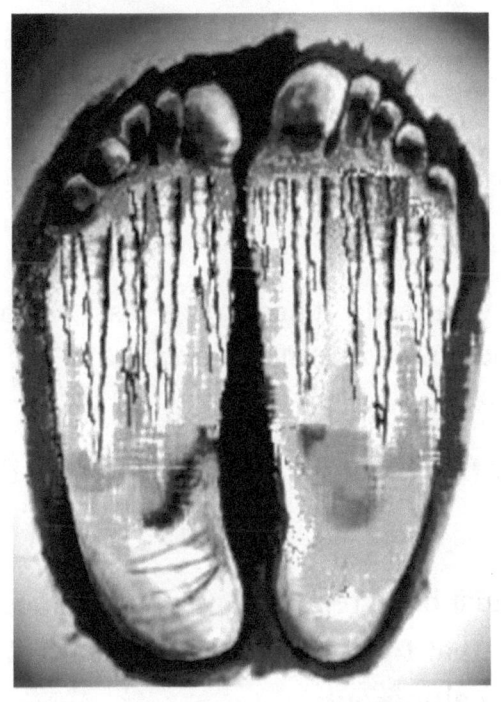

and we all know how difficult it is to sleep
when one's feet have turned into icicles.
But, this night was different from all the rest.
It was a very special night ... yes it was ...
this night that I met a dog named
Rush Limbaugh.

5

As I have already stated, I was fast asleep,
but something woke me! It must have been Rush
calling-out:

"HTAED! HTAED! ARE YOU THERE?"

Rush must have repeated it several times for when I
realized that I was fully awake I heard Rush, very
plainly, calling-out:

"HTAED! HTAED! ARE YOU THERE?"

At first, something else I have already told
you, I was startled and afraid. After all it was
in the dead of the night, and everyone was sleeping
except for me — and there I was awake and all alone.
Rush was calling from outside my window.
I had left the window open because, as I
have already told you, it was such a nice night.

It was very pleasant falling asleep while being serenaded by the crickets and tree frogs — especially the crickets ... they always sing the same beautiful song.

(Whenever I hear a cricket sing I think back to this night.)

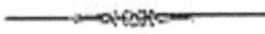

– 3 –

Crickets, I have found after long observations, are strictly nocturnal creatures. Although, occasionally, one does see or hear a cricket during the daytime.

Crickets, according to the dictionary:

"... Are insects with long antennae, the male

of which makes a chirping sound by the rubbing

together of the fore wings: it inhabits dry walls."

The dictionary failed to record my observation about crickets being, for the most part, nocturnal creatures.
I have also noticed that when one approaches

an area where there is a cricket, or
crickets chirping, he, or they will immediately
stop chirping. You may think that this is trivial
information ... it is not.
That night that I heard Rush calling —
I recall that the crickets were chirping. They were
chirping in spite of Rush's presence.

I have often thought of this over the years.
The only conclusion that I can derive at is that
Rush, being no ordinary creature, was sincerely
friendly toward the crickets . . .
and somehow, I believe, the crickets knew this.

I also think, though I really can not prove it,
that the crickets were happy that Rush was there ...
and, that they were communicating their pleasure to
him — in cricket language of course.

I hope that this, the information that crickets
communicate, does not surprise you. All living
creatures communicate to others in their species.
Most of us do not understand what they are
saying — the reason for this being that we
never took the time to learn their different languages.

You will also learn, if you are not
already aware of the fact, that most schools

only offer courses in human languages.
(I sometimes wish that someone had taken the
time to learn and record at least some of the
other creature's languages, so that people like us
could communicate with creatures other than
human beings, whenever we wanted to of course.
People are, sometimes, very hard to understand, which
makes it very hard to converse with them.
They, more often than not, do all of the talking
and no listening. This always makes the conversation
one-sided and very boring.)

Just think of how much fun it would be
to converse with a cricket, or cat, or a tree frog
or a bird. I know that they would have many
interesting stories to tell and many interesting things
to relate — not like some people.

– 4 –

Take Rush for instance, when first I saw
him I was not sure what Rush was. Rush looked
like a person, a truly magnificent person, but
there was something about Rush — when first I
saw him — that made me feel that he was not
a person. I felt that he was more than just a person.

(You can probably see this too — just by looking at
the picture of Rush. [In the following illustration].

The illustration, or drawing if you wish, is only a
rendering that was made from memory. I do hope that
I did Rush justice.
And I also hope that you can see in Rush what I
saw — at first glance that is.)
Rush was truly a magnificent creature.

His black hair was like no hair that I have
ever seen. It was long and silky, yet coarse in texture.
It hung 'round his head in loops and swirls.
It was perfectly kept — not a hair was misplaced.

I once asked him:
"How do you keep your hair so perfect?"

He replied:
"It is naturally this way. I never have to worry
about it ....
it never needs cutting, or washing, or combing.
It has always been this way for as long as I
can remember."

"How wonderful", I thought, "never to
have to worry about one's hair."

And his attire! This too was very unusual.
He was wearing a robe like no other that I
have seen. It was cut low about the neck — so
not to interfere with his hair, I believe — and
it draped his entire body. It was black and
white, with strange patterns embroidered all over it.
(Somewhat like those seen on costumes worn
by magicians.)

It touched the ground as light as a feather
and flowed to a point in the front and in the back.

Even more strange, was the fact that it
had no sleeves for his arms — if indeed he
did have arms, or feet for that matter.
I questioned him about this — after I had
complimented him on his exquisite taste of dress:

"Why are there no sleeves on your robe for your
arms?"

He smiled and said:
"I have no need for sleeves because —"

"No need for sleeves!", I remember saying, somewhat
astonished and excited.

"But —"

"I do everything with my mind little friend.",
he said affirmatively.

———————

– 5 –

"No," came a reply to Rush's inquiry, "it's Dick and Jayne!"

"What could be going on out there?", I thought to myself.
"Here it is in the dead of night and I am hearing all these people moving about outside."

"How wonderful!", Came the reply from the voice that had waken me.

(That voice I later recognized as belonging to Rush.)

"Please wait! I would like to speak with you.", the voice called-out again.

The curiosity of the goings-on outside over came my fright. I slowly approached the window until I could see three figures grouped together on our back lawn.

"What is going on out there?", I thought to myself again — somewhat perplexed.
Being naturally curious I was determined to man this post until I got to the bottom of this ....

So I prepared myself:
I rested my arms on the windowsill, and
my chin on my hands, and watched and
listened to this strange happening — with undaunted
intensity, of course.

I noticed that there was this magnificent creature,
Rush, a young man, named Dick and a young woman,
named Jayne.
As close as I can remember, as I have
already told you I do pride myself on my memory so I
do remember most of their conversation, I will relate
to you the minutes of their perplexing yet interesting

meeting.

———————

It began with the young man, Dick, addressing
himself to Rush.
(It appeared to me, by Dick's tone, that he
had met Rush at an earlier time in his life —
but, [somewhat confusing], he did not recognize him
… for that sake neither did Jayne, when first they
confronted each other):

———————

Dick: Who are you?

Jayne: Yes, who are you — or should I say …
What are you?

Rush: I am an echo of truths that were shouted
in your beginning.

I am the innocence of a child's mind ...
a small hand — mute,
preciously clutching a wilting flower.

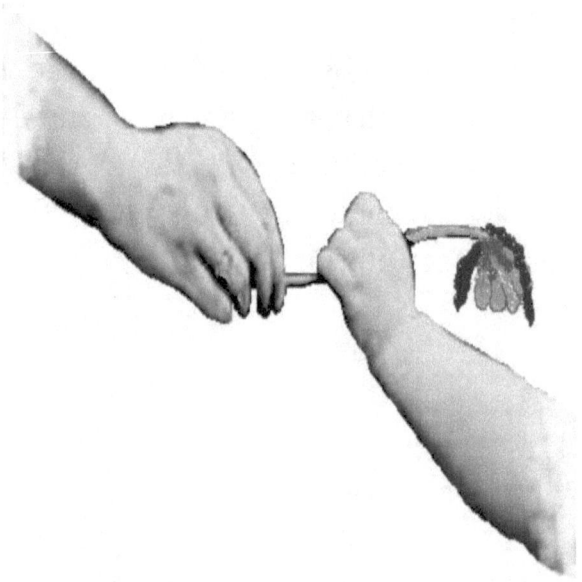

I am your past directing your future.
I am you.

My name is Rush.

Dick: What are you doing here?

Jayne: And why did you want to speak with us?

Rush: I am here because I am at home.
As you can see it is a realm void of sense ....
It is a world where one must exist by thought.
I wanted to speak with you because I
wanted to answer your questions.

Everyone who enters the night is seeking
answers to questions ...
questions that were created during the day.

———————

Dick: Rush, why did you say that you were me?

Jayne: And at the same time say that you were
me?

Rush: Simply because I have experienced
situations and things similar, if not
the same, as those that you have.
And, since we are all products of our
experiences, I am, in fact, a part of both of you ...
as you both are a part of me.
I am, and I was a dog ...
that you called "Rush Limbaugh".

––––––––––

Dick: Rush Limbaugh?!
The same Rush Limbaugh as when we were
children?

Jayne: Our dog Rush Limbaugh?
You're our black and white dog?
But —

Rush: I am that friend that you speak of.
But in my world I exist in a form unthought-of by
you.

Unfortunately, at the time of our last meeting
our means of communication was very limited ...
and therefore, was just basically informative.

Time has changed us ...
but I trust that our friendship has endured.
I look upon you as being very special in my past
life.
It was you and your love that started me
on a path which led to peace.

—————————

Dick: But, I still don't understand any of this ...
Please forgive me ... I think?

Jayne: You'll have to forgive us Rush,
we've had a very trying day.
I'm sure that you're telling us the truth.

Rush: My quest for general knowledge led me to
a gained knowledge — truth was a part of this

gained knowledge.

It has also given me peace and tranquility.
Gained knowledge freed me so that I could be
an eternal entity.

— —

With this in mind I ask ...
Why are you so troubled?

———————

Dick: I just don't know ...
about anything anymore, Rush.
It seems that when I finally reach a
point where everything is going good —
BAM ... the bottom falls out!

Jayne: Someone else got the promotion that
Dick wanted. It would have solved all of our
problems ...
And he worked so hard for it.

Rush: You have my sympathy ... but,
if I may, Dick obviously did not work hard
enough.
Had he convincingly wanted it
he would, at this moment, have it.
Consider yourself fortunate then to have
experienced this situation. There is an important
lesson to be gained from this:
"excellence" — does not happen by accident.

———————

Dick: Rush, I try and I try and it just
seems as though I can't get anywhere!
I feel like giving it all up.

Rush: Your losing this opportunity to fulfill a
want is not as important as your failing
to gain constructive knowledge from its
existence.
You have failed in the proper use of your
reasoning.

Your concern with the past fact that you
lost and your temporal loss of dreams indicates
that you are more involved with fantasy than you
are with reality.

You, unfortunately, were never properly taught
how to use your gift of learning to find inner
peace.

———

Dick: Sometimes I get so depressed that I think
that there's only one way out ... simply end it all.

Rush: To end it all is the worst possible thing
that you could ever do.
This action that you speak of leads to total loss
....
You would disrupt your cycle and be lost
from this reality forever. — So unnecessary.

Whenever you feel this depressed seek out help.
There is help waiting — find it ...

and find the good.
Look for the knowledge. Look so that you can
prevent this pain from ever happening again.

If you are troubled turn to me.

————————

Jayne: How can you — Rush — our
dog, tell us people, human beings, that we are
doing wrong?!
What do you know?

Rush: I know what I have experienced.
Do you think that it was easy for me, a dog,
to achieve divinity? I was an outcast ...

I was a dog!
My struggle was up a mountain of cascading
boulders but I never gave up.

I never considered defeat — I knew that
I could achieve my goal because I was

determined to achieve it!

The harder it became — the more determined
I became ....
I knew that in the end I would win
and I learned that the harder it was to reach
the pinnacle — the greater the joy would be
when I did.

I am very thankful that my quest was an almost
impossible dream — for I learned much
on my journey.
I learned what was needed to succeed.

It was not until I realized the good in my failures
that I began to excel.

———————

Dick: It's not easy, Rush.
I find myself faced with difficult decisions.

Sacrifices — that I'm not willing to make ...

that I cannot make!

Rush: Dick, I looked!

I looked until my eyes teared from pain ...
until I could no longer see ...

Then, I listened until my ears were
deafened — forever silent.

But still I went on ...
feeling for my goal — feeling until my touch
was numb.

I then used my sense of smell until it
too was no more.

Yet, I would not consider defeat ...

I still had my sense of taste — it was
all that I had left, but I was committed ...
and what good was it to me four-fifths dead ...
I continued.

— —

The results of my determination are visible ...
success was but a lick away.

———————

Jayne: But sometimes one has no way of
knowing whether or not what one must sacrifice
will be in vain ...
or, if the sacrifice is really needed.

Rush: You must fully commit yourself to any
task that you undertake!

I sacrificed my physical existence in
order to achieve total knowledge ...
I had no way of knowing if my goal
could be reached ...

but I knew that it was what I wanted
and I was determined not only to try,
but to succeed.

— —

If you can dream ...
you can attain.

———————

Dick: Words!
Just words, Rush!
They're easy for you to say ...
Look at you!
Now look at me!
If it's not my own lack of confidence it's
the lack of confidence that everyone else
displays toward me.

Rush: Look into my mind ...
look at all of the scars.
Look at what I had to over-come!

Do you think that it was easy for me?
Do you actually think that it was easy for
a dog to make it in a people's world?!

I too cried ...
I too felt the pain that you are feeling.
But I refused to give-up ...
No matter how hard they laughed.
I choked on my tears and said nothing.

— —

I, too, learned from their mistakes.
I learned that in any two person conflict that
there was a third person profit to be made
and I used this enlightenment to help me attain
my goal.

————

Dick: Rush, I want to win ...

I want to win more than anything else in the
world.
What good am I to anyone if all I do is fail ...?
You can't eat failures.

Rush: You cannot eat success either.
Your failures are exposing you to an aspect
of life which is vital for life itself.
In order to win, the way you want ...
in order to fulfill your dreams ...
you must first lose (not on purpose).

You must lose in order to gain the knowledge
of the experience.

What joy can you derive from winning if
to win is meaningless, which is the case if you
have never been exposed to losing.

———————

In retrospect — our failures are just trials
... and all trials are accompanied by tears.

A winner tears because at some point in
life he or she has lost and has struggled to
cope with this past failure ...
these tears are the shedding of all the pain.

A loser tears because he/she
feels that the loss is forever the present.

The loser has not yet learned that there is
knowledge in this loss, knowledge which
he/she must gain in order to become a winner ...
he/she has not yet learned — "fortitude".

— —

Their tears are the same ...
only their expressions are different.

————

Jayne: But, Rush ...

What about those of us who are handicapped?
What about we people who are not fortunate
enough to have the necessary equipment
to attain our goal?

Rush: Those who appear to be the most deprived on the Earth are, in fact, the most fortunate ...
they are positioned for maximum gain.
But, unless they recognize this and act accordingly they will remain losers in the eyes of those who judge them to be such.
Besides ... all goals are different ...
only the remoteness from the goal is the determining factor as to the work required.

— —

The farther you are from your goal — the more rewarding your life will be when you reach it ...
and you will, if you are sincere with yourself.

———

Life is a wondrous state of being.
Be thankful for the life you have —
whether it be full or in part.

Take dedicated advantage of whatever knowledge you can find and use it to gain betterment — for yourself and all life in general.

Again:
The greater the odds you face
the greater the success you can win.

Remember too:
Respect your obligations and show gratitude
for unexpected helpful blessings.

— —

Foremost to remember in your endeavors is that
only good reciprocates good.

———

Jayne: Like Dick, I sometimes experience bad
times and become very frustrated because
my environment seems out of control.
Sometimes, I'm irritable and take my troubles out
on those that I love ....
Sometimes, I unthinkingly hurt those who are
close to me when I sincerely don't mean to.

Rush: I have seen that many people react
this way when they are troubled.
It is during these periods of frustration
that the people around you need to be
understanding ...
an act based upon accepting and forgiving.

We must rely on one another for help.
We must rely on one another to share
the gained knowledge that accompanies scars.

— —

In the world in which we live, an ocean of love
without waves is not logical, nor is it real.

———————

Jayne: Rush, what's it all about?
The good ? ...
The bad? ...
Life? ...
Death?

Is it all just a random happening or is there something to it all? Something we seem to be unaware of or something we've just overlooked? Do you know the answer, Rush?

Rush: The answer is quite simple:
It all exists for you.
It is your good fortune ....
It is your reward for something yet unknown.
It is a wonderland where you are master of

 the dreams.

You — can make it heaven or hell
or anywhere in between.

— —

Logic dictates that if you can prove your ability to gain knowledge and use that knowledge to improve the quality of life around you — in a manner that is holy to life, respectful —
your rewards will be boundless and infinite.

You will have succeeded in attaining a goal that
is vaguely apparent to you ...
but one that (known or unknown to you) exists.

To be sure:
Nothing lasts forever — as only nothing ...
but you, a something, is a something
which can never be nothing — and therefore
will always be.

———————

If you are lacking a long-term goal
in your life ... if you, at this time, are uncertain of
your direction:

I challenge you ...
I challenge you to find the good in all of your
problems, to learn as much as you possibly can.
I challenge you to create harmony ...
to do good while striving to be better or the best.

— —

I challenge you to be greater than me — a dog ...
a dog named Rush Limbaugh.

– 6 –

I visualized thousands of creatures like Rush,
all mysteriously moving about in the darkness,
looking for Htaed.

I saw Htaed as being an elusive shadow hiding
in the darkness of the night.
(Everyone knows that you can not see a shadow in the
dark.)

How funny I thought this was ...
looking for a shadow in the dark. It was like
playing hide-and-go-seek with no one playing.

"All they need is a light.", I concluded, "Everyone
knows that in order to see one's shadow all one need
do is stand in front of a light and look behind them —
in the opposite direction."

How proud I was of myself to have thought
of the solution for finding Htaed, but my solution was
good only if Htaed, indeed, was a shadow.
Since I had no way of knowing I could only speculate.

It was fun to think of what could be
in the center of the night.

———————

"That's probably where Rush comes from,", I figured
...
"the center of the night.
There just has to be such a place!", I mused,
"It's only logical."
I recall from one of my science classes that the
Earth travels around the Sun, (completing one
full cycle every 365 days), and at the same
time it (the Earth) spins around on an imaginary axis,
(completing one full cycle every 24 hours) .
This is why there is day and night.
On one half of the Earth it's always day
and on the other side it's always night.

If you're on the side facing the Sun — it's day ...
and if you're on the opposite side, facing away,
in the shadow — it's night.

In the middle of the shadow is the

center of the night. And once everyday (the
twenty-four hour cycle) we pass through that center.

I calculated that since the Sun had set
at 8:23 o'clock last night and remembering
that the weather-person, on television, said that the
sunrise would be at 5:13 o'clock the next morning ...

I would be in the center of the shadow at
12:48 o'clock — very close to midnight.

How smart I was for figuring this out
without the help of anyone else.

I anxiously looked at my clock to see what
time it was. The clock read 2:30.
"My! This night is going by very fast", I
thought, "and how interesting it is."
How pleasant this night is as compared to all
the rest that I spent sleeping. The night is
surely as enjoyable as the day. It is sad to think
of all of the people who, like I was, are afraid of
the night.", I considered ... reflectively.

I wondered about all of the happenings
that had taken place during all of the previous
nights that had passed. I wondered about all
of the things that I had missed that go on
in the dark of night.

There could be so, so
many things that happen during the dead of the night.

There could be things that exist far beyond
the dreams of sleep.

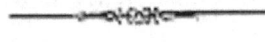

– 7 –

Sudden, loud claps of thunder and a lashing
wind woke me from my contemplations.
I looked at the clock again:
It read 2:59.

A storm was moving in.
I had consciously lost track of the time.
I instinctively turned back to the window —
fearing that I had missed something. Unfortunately, I
had.
Dick and Jayne had departed — but Rush was
still there.
I felt very sad that I could not have
watched Dick and Jayne's departure — at least to see

which way they went.

Now that I look back upon it
I suppose that it really does not matter
since I never saw from what direction they came.
But Rush was still there!

"He is far from home," I speculated, "if indeed
he did come from the center of the night."

"He is already two hours and fifty-nine
minutes away — according to my calculations."
I wondered if he realized where he was.
I wondered if I should tell him ...
I pondered this situation very carefully.
"One should always think before one acts!"
(This helpful information was taught to me
very early in life by an astute old gentle–
man, who I shall save for another tale.)

So — I thought, and thought and thought that I
should tell him. Besides, I truly wanted to
converse with him.

– 8 –

"**R**ush!" I yelled.

"Rush!
It's 2:59!"

(But of course by then it was 3 o'clock.)

I had forgotten that everyone else was asleep.
I turned toward my door and listened — to
hear if I had awakened anyone. Much to my
relief everyone was still silent.
How could I explain to my parents, who believed that
someone my age should really be asleep at this time,
all of the events that had happened. And how could I
explain my being awake at such an ungodly hour.
My parents would probably be very angry with
me for not being asleep. They were always strict about
my being in bed and asleep at precisely the time that
they wished me to be .... And here it was 3 o'clock —
and in the dead of the night.

I turned back toward the opened window —
and was frightened half to death!

There was Rush — staring at me! He
could not have been more than a foot away.

I must have been a very funny sight to him ...
I felt white as a ghost and felt my hair
standing on end.

Rush, very amused, burst into laughter.
Fortunately, thunder from the approaching
storm drowned-out his bellowing.

He quickly regained his stately composure and
promptly apologized for laughing at me.
"I am truly sorry for laughing at you. I did not mean to
insult you …
but you did look very comical."

"You frightened me!" I said. "This is the
first time, for as long as I can remember, that
I have been awake this late at night. Besides,
you knew that you were there — but I did not!"

"And why are you not sleeping like everyone else?",
he asked.

"Because your calling woke me.", I said.

"I apologize for that too, but are you sure
that you are awake?", he asked.

"Yes! I must be." I said, "You yourself just
inquired as to why I was awake."

"As you wish.", he said.

"Where are you from?", I asked. (I was curious
to see if my theory was correct.)

"I am from a place pronounced:
sy-chy-wat, and spelled:

S-I-H-C-I-H-W-T-A-H-T.

It is opposite a place pronounced:
ton-sy-chy-wat, and spelled:

T-O-N-S-I-H-C-I-H-W-T-A-H-T."

I was unsatisfied with his answer because
it did not inform as to whether my calculations
were right or wrong.

"I have never heard of either place", I said —
somewhat indignant.

"Of course not", he said, "you are to young
to conceive either of these two places."

He paused for a moment. It appeared to me that he
was deliberating — wanting to add further
information.

Finally, he said:
"Sihcihwtaht is in the center of the day.
Tonsihcihwtaht is in the center of the night. They
both exist twenty-four hours a day and both happen

everywhere ...
but neither happen at the same place at the same
time — although they both do exist at the same
time and during the course of the day they both
end-up existing in the same spot."

"You are confusing me.", I said.

"Someday you will understand — most everyone
does.", Rush said reassuringly.

All of this did not make much sense to me —
only that I wanted to be right ...
that he was from the center of the night.

"I surmise that you are far from home.", I
said to him — trying to display my intellectual
maturity.

"That depends upon which direction I travel.",
he answered.
"If I go one way I am nine hours away. If I
choose to go in the opposite direction I am fifteen
hours away from where I began ...
and, anyway, if I choose to go nowhere
I will be home eventually.
I have three choices — but only two directions."

"Again, you are confusing me.", I said.

"No I am not — you are confusing yourself.", he said.

"You are not thinking ...
you are just listening. Perhaps someday you will
understand."

– 9 –

"**W**ho is Htaed?" I asked.

"Htaed!", he said in a chuckle, "You should
not concern yourself with such a matter. One as
young as you should be more interested in things that
inhabit your boundless world."

"You should be interested in why crickets chirp, and
why they look as they do. And why there are so many
different kinds of plants, and what each one's function
is ... and how each
natural thing can benefit you — they all can.

There are so many things yet unknown, or
lost in time, that it will be all of your lifetime
before even a small percentage of them are
explained or rediscovered and recorded."

"But what about Htaed?", I asked.

"Htaed", Rush said, "is a natural actor of whom many
know nothing about.
Accept the knowledge that Htaed exists, and therefore
is not non-existent as many believe. Htaed is nothing
to be apprehensive about — unless you fear the
unknown."

"Why is that?", I asked — listening very intently to
every word he said.

"Before this night you feared the dark
but see how interesting it has been for you.
Perhaps you did not understand everything
that was said during my conversation with
Dick and Jayne,
but I am sure that if you retain part of what
was said, and review it often, that you will
continue and prosper with contentment and
assurance.

You will learn that many, many things in

life are confusing and distressing. Try not to
let them depress you or frustrate you as
it will all make sense in the passing of time.

Dear little friend, if ever you find yourself
confronted by such a situation
use the 'Spell of Words'. It will, sometimes, help you
to resolve your troubles."

"What is the 'Spell of Words' Rush? I have
never heard of that.", I said searchingly.

"They are special words uttered during times of stress.
An example of these very special words reads
like this:

Trouble and problems I do face.

Sha – Ha – Indy – Talace!

If I am good, honest and true ...

All will turn bright — opposite of blue.

This 'Spell of Words', you must not forget, must be
said the moment that you are confronted with a feeling
of depression. Remember — before you do

anything else ... Say the 'Spell of Words' ...
to yourself — do not scream them as many people
do."

"I will remember. I will Rush."

––––––––––

To this day I have remembered the 'Spell of Words'.
And, I have remembered to repeat them every time
that I have been confronted with a situation that I felt
warranted their being said. (I must say, at this time,
that they sometimes help; at least I have found them to
help. I suppose that it depends entirely upon when and
where they are used.)

Every time that I am disturbed, I say:

"Trouble and problems I do face.
Sha – Ha – Indy – Talace!
If I am good, honest and true...
All will turn bright — opposite of blue."

– 10 –

"**A**re you positive you are awake?", he asked.

"Yes — quite positive.", I said.

"Well then, would you care to see a glimpse of Htaed?" he questioned me in a mysterious voice. "I believe that he is close enough to experience."

I was very curious to see who Htaed was — after all, it was because of Htaed that all of this began.

———————

"Oh, yes!", I said. "But do you think that he
will be disturbed?"

"I will let you view him from a distance — for
as I have said, you are too young. And it is because of
this, your being so young, that you must not touch him
— in any way. Remember please — just look! You
must promise me two things before we leave ..."

"Two things?", I questioned.

"Yes.", he replied.
"First, that you will ask no questions. And second,
that you do not touch anything that you see."

"I promise you, Rush."

"Good," he said, "we will go before it starts to rain.
Close your eyes and follow my voice
it will lead you near — but only near enough
to encounter. You must never touch .."

You must never touch ...

You must never touch ...
You must never touch ...."

My eyes were closed and my mind was
pursuing Rush's voice. His voice slowly trans–
formed into a drone — a low buzzing sound:
sweet and melodious.

– 11 –

Somewhere in the distance I heard a roll of
thunder. It must have been the storm moving overhead
...
it sounded miles away.

"Rush," I softly called-out, "Rush!"

He answered in a whisper, "I am here.
I am here."

"Look — quick!", He said with a low breath.

I opened my eyes as fast as I could — fast
enough to catch sight of a flash of red ...
Then a flash of green ...
Then a flash of yellow ...
Then blue ...
Orange.

"That is Htaed's trail ...
We are getting very close.", Rush whispered.

The colors vanished as sudden as they appeared.
Awed, I tried desperately to focus on a familiar object.
I soon realized that I was no longer in my room.
"Where could I be?", I asked myself, "Where?!"
I saw nothing but glittering lights — far off in the
distance they were all around — encased in darkness.

"Could I be in space?
Could I be in outer space?!", I asked myself.
"Or ...
perhaps ...
the center of the night?"

I vainly looked for Rush — but I could not see him anywhere. I looked up and down and all around.

"Rush!", I called, "Rush! Where are you?!"

Again the whisper:

"Be at peace little friend, I am here."

"But why can I not see you?"

"No questions — remember."

"But ..."

"Shhh! Listen to the sounds."

I strained my begging ears to hear sounds far off in the distance:

"*pitta-patta, pitta-patta, pitta-patta, pitta-patta ...*"

It sounded like a thousand little drums:

"*pitta-patta, pitta-patta, pitta-patta, pitta-patta ...*"

A flash of Red ..

A flash of green ...

A flash of yellow ...
And all was normal again.

- *12* -

I watched the stars twinkling:
gold and white — soft and bright.
The blackness of space, which surrounded me,
felt soothing and cool.
I began to feel the presence of something unknown
and I could no longer hear the thousand little drums.

The colors flashed again — but this time the
red was last to show, It lingered on
and it slowly, in a rhythmic fashion, began to take on a
shape — a very indistinguishable shape.

(I can safely say that it did not look like anything that
I have ever seen before.)

"*Ho! Ho! Ho!*", it bellowed out.

"*Ho! Ho! Ho!*"

How fascinating, I thought, is this strange, large, red blob of a shape that dances like jello and bellows out:

Ho! Ho! Ho!"

Could this be Htaed?, I wondered, Could this be what Rush was looking for?
No sooner had I thought this than the strange,

large, red blob of a shape that danced like
jello burst into a dull green and melted into
what seemed to be, of all things, a palm tree.

It quivered and shook — jumped up and
down, and began shouting-out:
"Watch-out for Sunday! Watch-out for Sunday!

Watch-out for Sunday! ... "

"What a queer tree.",
I mumbled, to no one in particular.
"I have never, never in my whole life ever
seen a talking tree! And such an excited one
at that!"

I remembered that I had promised Rush that
I would not ask any questions — and I had
been cautioned about it.

"Well", I thought, "at least I can make statements."

———————

"You are such a queer tree.", I said — hoping
that this would insult it and irk it into
telling me what it really was, and why it
was here ...
not to mention why I should watch-out for Sunday.

"I have never seen a tree like you."

"You won't see me on Sunday!", it yelled back.
 "Not on Sunday! Watch-out for Sunday!
Watch-out for Sunday! Watch-out for Sunday! ..."

"Why Sunday?", I thought to myself, "Why
is this silly tree so paranoid about Sunday?"
I knew that I could not ask why. Yet, do
to my overwhelming curiosity, I had to think of
a way to get it to tell me about Sunday —
without asking it a question ....

I thought, and thought and thought that if
perhaps I told it how much I enjoyed Sunday
"Yes", I considered, "this is the solution to my
problem!"

"Oh, Sunday", I said casually, "everyday should be
Sunday. It is the most wonderful day of the week.
Actually ... it is the best day ever.
I do wish that everyday were Sunday."

―――――――

"Sunday! Sunday!", it yelled — quivering
and shaking more than ever.
"Are you crazy?!", it screamed, "That will
be the day that they strip me of my palms!"
"They will leave me barren, seedless ...
naked to the world!"

With that said it began to shake violently ...
Its' mane of palms became nothing but a blur
against the black background of space.
Suddenly — it shouted,

"Hurricane!
Hurricane!"

And then — POOF ...

It vanished.

"Certainly that could not have been Htaed!",
I grumbled.
"Not that silly paranoid tree."
"How absurd it is for me to even think that
Rush would be looking for that — that stupid tree."
I wondered where it went to. I pondered this ....

"At least the strange, large, red blob of a shape
did not disappear without leaving a trace." I thought.
"Maybe there is a track around here that
will lead me to an explanation for all of this nonsense
....
After all, every mystery contains a clue, some of
which are more obvious than others", I thought.
"Maybe the clue that I am seeking is barely visible."

With this in mind, I began examining the
area of space where the queer tree had appeared.
Upon close examination I discovered a very,
very small yellow dot ... perhaps I should say
"sphere," which is a more accurate description.
It looked to be about the size of a tiny

pea — it was very hard to locate because
it blended into the background of stars.

I believe that this was an act of camouflage.
I examined this very, very small sphere
from all sides. I detected, with my naked eye
and much concentration, that it was pulsating,
throbbing.
"Strange", I thought, "all of the apparitions
that I have seen so far, in some way or another, have
been moving."

I focused on this very, very small yellow
sphere for what seemed to be ages. I finally
grew bored with watching it pulsate. It seemed
to me that that was all that it did — pulsate.
I knew that it was time for another statement:

"Little, yellow, pulsating spheres are surely **boring to
watch**.", I said — in a very disgusted tone.
(I really did not mean to offend the very small yellow
sphere. I had realized since my encounter with the
crazy palm tree that it is very wrong to unjustly cause
undue pain.
Somehow this moral thought had developed in
my mind without my being conscious of it.)
The small yellow sphere completely ignored my
statement and just continued to pulsate without
change.
I felt guilty for the way that I had insulted
it. I knew that I had to make amends,

"Small yellow sphere ...
I sincerely apologize for insulting you. Please
forgive me I mean you no discourtesy."

No sooner had the last word left my

mouth than the small yellow sphere exploded
into a billion, billion tiny yellow spheres.
Each tiny yellow sphere was speeding on a path away
from the point where once the very small yellow
sphere had existed ... all speeding outward ...
and, at the same time, each was speeding on
a path that appeared to be arcing, in relation to the
point where once the small yellow sphere existed.

Each tiny yellow sphere was, at the same time, trailing
yellow light. They light-up the black space for as far
as I could see.
Smaller and smaller they became as they sped away.
Farther and farther ...
Smaller and smaller —
until everything was black again.

"Oh, I do hope that I did not say anything wrong!",
I said out-loud, "I meant no wrong-doing."
Well — no sooner were the tiny billion, billion
spheres not visible, than they became visible again.
They looked to be on the exact same paths as
before — only in reverse.

Closer and closer ...
Larger and larger — until they all collided, at
the same time, in the exact space where once
there was the small yellow sphere. And there, again,
was the small yellow dot ...
Just as it was when first I saw it.
Needless to say, (since then I have learned that
everything exists in cycles), it began all over again —
exactly as it had minutes earlier.

"Rush!", I whispered, "I know that you are still
here — even though I can not see you."

"Yes, I am." came the reply from nowhere, "I am still with you."

"Tell me about the small yellow sphere."

"It is alive like you and I.", he said.

"Its' cycle is its' life.
Its' motion is its' breath.
Its' mass is its' substance ...

It will always be contained, because all of its parts always return to their original point of departure.
For every tiny yellow sphere speeding on its path there is another tiny yellow sphere speeding on an opposite path ...
Their distance from the point of departure is always equal.
It is because of this balanced relationship
that when all of these tiny yellow spheres collide, for that instance, they make the small yellow sphere.
And it is at this time and at this point that the small yellow sphere exists, again, as the
small yellow sphere — as you know it to be.

But, mind you, it still exists as the small
yellow sphere even when it has exploded into the
billion, billion tiny yellow spheres. It exists because,
(something you have probably learned in school):

A whole is made up of the sum of its' parts.

All of these parts, the tiny billion, billion yellow
spheres, are part of the cycle in the existence of the
small yellow sphere. It is because of this that I made
you promise not to touch anything."

"I do not understand, Rush", I said,
in no particular direction.

"If you were to interfere with the cycle of
just one of these billion, billion tiny yellow spheres ...
if you where to touch just one and deflect it
from its preordained path you would destroy
the existence of the small yellow sphere.

That one missing sphere would change the
course of all of the others when they again collided
and perhaps, (how sad it would be), that they, the

billion, billion minus one tiny yellow spheres, would end up in unbalanced paths — never to unite again as the small **yellow sphere**."

———————

"How truly sad.", Rush rejoined.
"How sad indeed", I sighed.

A moment of silence captured my inner space and for an instance I remember feeling nothing.

————◦⊹⊱⊰⊹◦————

"There is much to absorb in one's life, little
friend, and much to reflect upon.
Look behind you — and to the East", directed
Rush's voice.

I turned about and peered into the distance, far-off, I
noticed something approaching. It was
indistinguishable, but I could perceive that it was
floating toward me.
"I can not see what it is, Rush. It is too far away."

"Wait.", said Rush, "Wait and see."

I waited and stared, and still, even though the object
came near, I could not figure-out what it was.
It was nearly round; it looked to be about a foot
in diameter. It was shiny — tinted blue,
and it contained something gold — moving
about within it.
It looked very familiar, but I just could
not recognize it.

"I am sorry Rush", I said apologetically, "either it is still to distant or, it escapes me."

"Think back a few years ...
back in your life ...
back to a fish in a bowl.", Rush said.

"My pet goldfish!", I said, "It's my pet goldfish!"

I felt like crying ...

but I contained myself. I guess that I should
tell you why:

Once, many years before this incident, I
was given a goldfish, by one of my relatives,
as a present. I cherished this fish.
I protected it and I cared for all of its' needs.
It appreciated my existence, as I did its' existence —
we were friends.
I would sit and watch it for hours-on-end.

———————

I have always been very curious about other
living creatures and I study them whenever I
have the opportunity to do so.
We complemented each other very well.
The bowl, in which it lived, was set upon a
beautiful wooden stand, which I had made myself (I
had labored on that stand for at least three weeks. You
see ... I loved that fish ...
And the making of a beautiful wooden stand to
support its transparent world was the least I
could do, I felt, to show my love.)

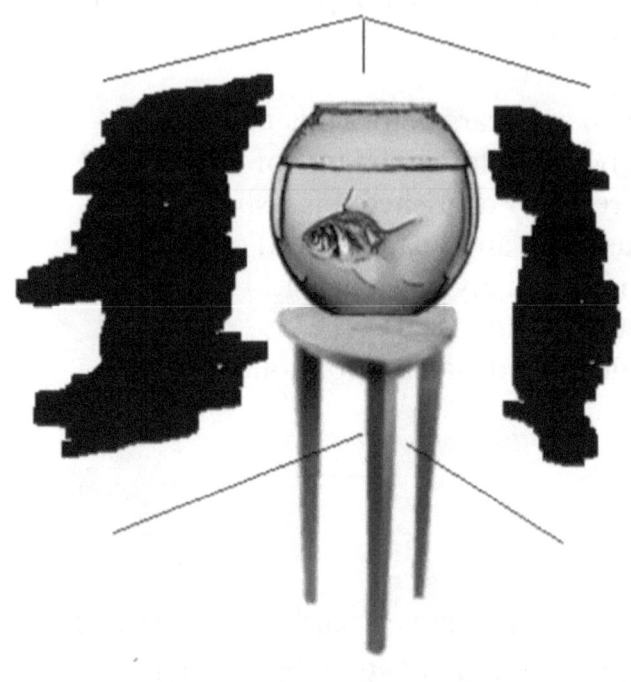

It was content with the life it led ...
until one day ... when I was away ...
our family dog was romping about in my
room and knocked-over the beautiful
wooden stand which supported the
transparent world of my dear, dear friend ....

Its' world shattered when the transparent globe hit the
floor and my friend — died.

I cried when I heard what had happened.
I was very sad ... and for the first time
in my life — I too wanted to die.
I wanted our family dog to die for what it
had done. I believed that it had purposely
knocked-over the stand because it was jealous ...
and nothing that anyone said could make me
believe otherwise.
It was a very long time before I forgave that dog,

I eventually realized that it had not
knocked-over the stand on purpose, and that I
was reacting from anxiety and self pity.
I have always felt very bad and guilty for
the way that I had neglected that dog for so long after
that incident ....

He was just a playful dog who meant no malice.
I had forgotten all about my pet goldfish.

– *14* –

"**R**ush," I remember saying, "Why did you
show me this?
What does my pet goldfish have to do with Htaed?"

I waited for an answer from Rush,
but no answer came ...
instead my straining ears heard:

"pitta-patta, pitta-patta, pitta-patta, pitta-patta ..."

"The thousand little drums.", I thought to myself.
"Rush?!", I strained my ears again, listening through
the thousand little drums, probing for that all-knowing
whisper.
But, again instead, my ears pick-up another
familiar sound:

"Chirp–chirp. Chirp–chirp. Chirp–chirp ..."

The black space around me was becoming
brighter. Light was filtering in from somewhere.
I still had not gotten an answer from Rush.
I began to become afraid and in a
blinding moment of panic, everything changed.

– 15 –

As I slowly came to my senses I became
aware of the fact that I was sitting-up in my bed.

I looked around, half amazed and somewhat dazed, not believing where I was.

I gazed at my opened window and through the dull light of early day, which was filling my room, I could see that it was raining outside.
The falling rain was pounding on the roof in a very familiar beat:

"*pitta-patta, pitta-patta, pitta-patta, pitta-patta ...*"

"The thousand little drums!", I said out-loud with a sense of information.
And then ...
I heard a cricket chirping:

"*Chirp–chirp. Chirp–chirp. Chirp–chirp ...*"

It sounded very near.
I looked all around, but could see nothing.
I noticed that the rain was falling into my room through my opened window
so I got-up out of bed and went to close it ...
all the while I was wondering about the things

that I had just previously experienced.
"Did I dream all of those things?"
I could remember everything so clearly.
"It could not have been a dream." I thought
to myself, "I just know it was not."
As I began closing the window I heard the
cricket again. He sounded very close — so close that I
knew that he was somewhere inside my room ...
and very near to me.
After closing the window I began examining the area
at hand.

"*Chirp–chirp. Chirp–chirp.*"

"There he goes again.", I mumbled.
"I wonder. I just wonder ..."
I pulled back the opened curtains and there,
sitting on the inside windowsill, was a cricket — the
largest cricket I have yet to see.
He must have been all of three inches long and
an inch high.
He was completely black — except for a large
white spot, which covered the front part of his head ...
like a white mask — it looked like face.

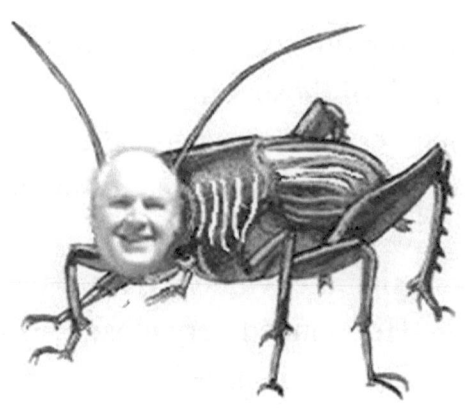

I stared at him, awed by his presence and appearance, and he stared back.
Suddenly, without provocation, he leaped upon my shoulder and began chirping.
Only what I heard was not what I was ac–customed to hearing — especially from a cricket. Instead of the usual:

"*Chirp–chirp. Chirp–chirp. Chirp–chirp* ..."

I heard a distinctive song. A quaint little song whose lyrics were:

Around and around,

and around it goes.

Its' cycle was set

a long time ago.

Night then day, and

day then night.

Light then dark, and

dark then light.

Around and around,

and around it goes...

If ever it will stop

no one knows.

"What a nice song.", I thought to myself,

"What a nice little song."

———————

His beautiful little song mellowed in my ears ...
and I am positive that, somewhere, in the melody I
heard, "I am here. I am here."

I felt Rush's presence and I felt at ease.
"I know now that what I have experienced I
have really experienced.", I said to myself.
I smiled — a knowing smile.

I climbed back into bed with my new
found friend still perched upon my shoulder.
I talked to that cricket as if he understood
every word I said ...
and that cricket chirped back as if he did!
"I will care for you for as long as you like,
my little friend.", I told it.
"I will find you a safe, dark box to live in,
and I will find food for you too ...
but most important of all I will be your friend."

"Chirp–chirp. Chirp–chirp. Chirp–chirp... ",

It answered.
It then commenced to serenade me to sleep.
Our friendship lasted a long time. We were
inseparable — that white faced cricket and me.

It would sing its' beautiful little song, and I would
laugh.
It would chirp, and I would feel alive ...
especially at night — when I would sleep.

– 16 –

Many years have passed since all of these events took place.
Many years too have passed since I last saw
my cricket.

(Allow me to correct myself, "My friend the
cricket."):
No creature should belong to another creature ...
not in the sense that one is the master and one is
the slave ...
that is, without the mutual consent of both parties
being given in accordance through freewill.
I wish that someday all creatures exist in a state of
friendship ... that they help one another with their
needs ....
that they do so not because of fear of punishment or
because of personal reward —
either material or physical.
And it is silly for me to insist that I own my dog ...
my dog has its own freewill and stays with

me because we are friends. And because
we are friends we provide for one another.
If it, through its' own discretion, chose to
leave me for another, or just to leave,
my chaining it to prevent its leaving would
make me a very selfish person ...
and make it a very miserable prisoner. Its'
happiness should override my selfishness unless
at the time it chose to leave it would be worst off,
mentally and/or physically ... then it would be my
obligation to protect my friend ... for the time being.

I always try to put myself into another
creature's position before I act toward, or react to, in
anyway, that creature.
I find that because of this attitude my
life continues with, what I believe to be, a minimum
of problems.

– 17 –

Every night, weather permitting, I walk for a
mile or two and think about all of the things
that I have, to date, experienced.

I find that there have been some unpleasant experiences, which I deem as being periods of learning and many, many pleasant ones (which I deem as being products of self applied knowledge).

I also listen to the crickets, when they are active, and think of how my life has developed from the point when first I was aware that crickets existed.
Or ... I sometimes just walk and daydream about being someone more grand than I am. Fortunately, I always manage to recapture reality and face the truth of my position ...

That I am someone special ...
I am because I exist. And I am aware of the fact that I can be anything that I want to be (if given the chance to do so).

How lucky I am to be given this opportunity ... that is, to possess the knowledge that my future can be whatever I want it to be — be it a surprise or be it the attaining of a goal.

– 18 –

I remember too, Rush once telling me:
"If you travel a path from beginning to end
you have experienced only one-half of that path.

Every path has two directions --- two separate
experiences. Every path has two beginnings and
two endings.
It makes no difference which beginning you
choose — as long as you choose them both.

In order to gain the complete experience of
a path you, the traveler, must tread that path
three times ... (the third time is resuming your
travels).
Then, and only then, are you ready to continue onto
the next."

This statement has given me many hours of
entertainment. I often think about it and its meaning.
I suppose that Rush, in Rush's way, was
telling me something important about life —
as when Rush taught me the 'Spell of Words'.
I remember too Rush telling me,

"Water is the Earth's life blood —
respect it ... it holds your futures' future."

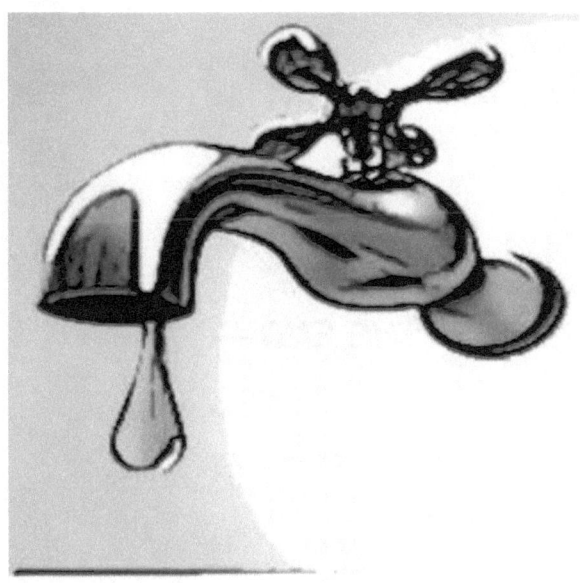

A prophetic truth ... I am sure of — it's something
I think of daily and practice likewise.
I learned much from Rush.
I learned so very much from my childhood friend.

— THE END —

A Dog Named Rush Limbaugh

ABOUT THE AUTHOR

M. A. Churchill was born and grew-up in the southern New England area. Molded by a very independent and curious nature. His secondary education was completed while attending several public and private schools; and thereafter attended several colleges, but never finding a challenge or fulfilling experience he left college and headed-out into world.
He entered the corporate world working in the computer department of one of the world's largest most diversified financial institutions. There he was a Main Frame Computer Console Operator and then a Technical Writer, working on internal documents (one of which seemed to violate the Anti Trust Act and led to his quitting the company in protest).

A Free Spirit, he eventually ended-up as a street vendor of flowers in one of the Capitol cities. This work suited him: self-employed, fifteen hour workweek, ample compensation and a constant array of customers (stories) from the Homeless to Movie Stars. It also afforded him the opportunity to indulgence in his passions of inventing, writing, creating, learning and living, which to this day he is still doing.

www.ingramcontent.com/pod-product-compliance
Lightning Source LLC
Chambersburg PA
CBHW020627130626
46552CB00003B/1108